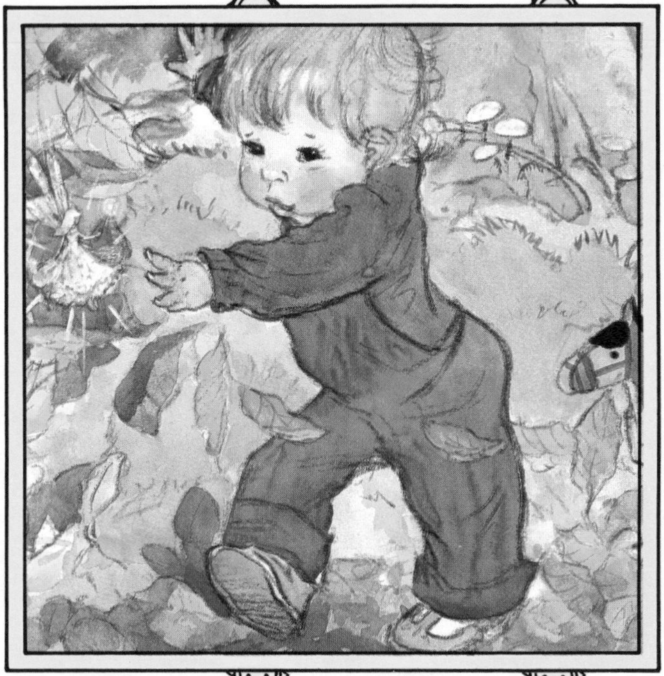

Sunshine Books™ is a trademark owned
by Modern Publishing, A Division of
Unisystems, Inc.
Printed in Belgium

BEST OF FRIENDS

ILLUSTRATED BY MARY BROOKS
TEXT ADAPTED BY JANE RESNICK
AND SUSAN POSTCANSER

Modern Publishing
A Division of Unisystems, Inc.
New York, New York 10022

THE HOPPITY BUNNY

Early one morning Casey and his little
sister Carrie went to feed their pet
bunny, Whirly, who lived in a
cage near the garden.
"Good morning, Whirly!" said Casey,
giving him a flower to eat.
Whirly licked Casey's finger and
seemed to smile at Carrie.
"Why don't we take her out for a
walk?" asked Carrie.
"No," said Casey. "Whirly is a
hoppity bunny. If we let her out,
she may run away."
But Carrie had already opened the
cage. Whirly hopped right out
and ran away. The children ran
after her. But as they got close,
Whirly hopped away again.
Sitting down to rest, Casey asked,
"What will we do? I miss Whirly."
Suddenly Whirly peeked out from
behind a tree. Then she hopped right
into Casey's arms. The hoppity little
bunny took another bite of Casey's
flowers. She was happy to be home!

SAMMY AND HAPPY

There was nothing in the world that
Sammy wanted more than his own little
happy puppy. His birthday seemed
so very far away. But finally it arrived,
and so did the puppy he had
been waiting for.
The puppy jumped out of his box.
Sammy giggled and played with his
brand new friend. "Now you need a
name," said Sammy. "But I just can't
think what your name should be.
Maybe I'll name you Nosey," said
Sammy. "You seem to put your
nose into everything." But the
puppy looked away. So
Sammy decided to think again.
"Maybe I'll name you Bouncer, and
then you can run and jump and play all
you want." But the puppy was resting
quietly beside Sammy and 'Bouncer'
didn't seem right at all.
"I know!" shouted Sammy, "I'll name
you Happy! And you'll always be near."
Happy wagged his tail, barked
and gave Sammy a big wet kiss!

THE BATH

Jenny and Jody and Tim couldn't
decide what to do next. It had been a
busy afternoon. First they drew space-
ships with Jenny's new super-duper
colored markers. Next they played
'Catch Me If You Can.' Then they
rode their tricycles around
and around the yard.
When they were all dizzy and lying on
the grass, Jenny said, "What next?"
Just then Max, their puppy, ran into the
yard, chasing a tiny butterfly.
"I know," said Jenny. "Let's give
Max a bubble bath."
They sprayed him with water and
poured shampoo over his soft fur. Jody
scrubbed him with a soft brush and
Jenny washed behind his ears.
"Time for your bath!" yelled their
Mommy from the back porch.
"We already had ours," laughed
the three children. "We took
ours with Max!"

FLOWERS AND BUGS

Sarah was picking flowers on a bright, sunny day. And right before her nose, just before she plucked a rose, out crawled a tiny little beetle. "Oooh," Sarah squealed as he marched across her toes, but she didn't move; she let it stay. The beetle kept walking. He crawled right back onto the rose! Then Sarah didn't notice, Sarah didn't see, that a caterpillar inched up to her knee. He was oh, so fuzzy and really very friendly, but he tickled as he moved and Sarah jumped. He tumbled to the ground, fell upside down, and Sarah saw him there. "Mr. Caterpillar," she said, "now, how are you going to get where you're going? Sarah watched him go, even though she wished that she could keep him.
Sarah watched the sun change the flowers' colors. Sarah liked the roses. She thought they were so pretty, but bugs were really much more fun!

THE SPECIAL FRIEND

Mandy was all dressed up in her
jumper. It had little flowers all over
and two big pockets. She was *not*
at all happy about it.
"I want to go outside," she cried. "I
can't run and jump in these clothes."
"It's just for Aunt Nettie's visit,"
said her mommy. "Please try
to stay neat today!"
Mandy felt very grumpy as she walked
down the garden path.
"Grrr-uph!" Mandy growled as she sat
down on a smooth, flat rock.
"Rrrib-it," answered a fat
frog at her feet.
"Hello, Fat Frog," said Mandy.
The frog smiled at Mandy and jumped
right into her pocket.
When Mandy came home, she kissed
her Aunt Nettie hello.
Suddenly, Fat Frog jumped out of her
pocket and on to Aunt Nettie's lap!
Everyone laughed as Fat Frog
hopped about!

THE BEST-FRIEND CAT

"Now I'm going to play with Tillie
and her little kitten," said Terry. "She's
the sweetest, best-friend cat
in the whole world!"
Tillie was sleeping under the porch.
"Come out, Tillie," said Terry. "I've
got big plans for you."
Terry dressed Tillie up in a lacy bonnet
and they had a pretend tea party.
Then they played mommy and baby.
Terry was the mommy, of course. She
carried Tillie all around the house and
then twice around the yard.
When Terry told Tillie they were going
to play rocket ship next, Tillie
scampered back under the porch. She
really needed her cat nap now!
"Don't worry," said Terry, calling after
her. "Tomorrow we'll play again." Tillie
yawned, happy to be under the porch
with her kitten like before.

PETER'S PUPPY

Peter's puppy was named Tops. Peter
knew that Tops was very special. If
Peter fell down, Tops would help
him back up. And when it was
bedtime, Tops would jump on
the bed, ready for sleep.
One day, Peter and Tops went for a
walk with Cleo the puppy next door. As
they strolled along they found
two little kittens. Peter named them
Milton and Nancy.
"Where do they live?" Peter asked.
Tops barked and pointed. The kittens
just cried. "Meow!"
Peter followed his puppy until they
came to a backyard fence. At the
bottom was a small hole, and inside a
big cat. "She's looking for those two
little kittens, I bet!" said Peter. "And
Tops, my fine puppy, you found them!"
Peter took the kittens back to their
Mommy. Then he hugged Tops and
called him his own special puppy.

THE BEST KIND OF DAY

Annie thought that warm, bright sunny
days were the very best kind of day. Her
favorite thing of all to do, was to take
her sister Lisa to the park.
Getting ready was half the fun and
Annie took extra special care that
everything was just right. She'd help
Lisa gather their favorite toys to put in
the baby carriage. Lisa always made
sure that Sam, their stuffed rabbit, got a
special seat in front. Annie checked
that they had their egg salad
sandwiches and that Oscar, the dog,
was coming along. When they got to
the park, Annie and Lisa would laugh
and play. They took turns on the swing,
rode the merry-go-round, and picked
beautiful flowers for mother. And when
it was time to go back home, Annie
would smile at Lisa and think that it
had been the very best kind of day!

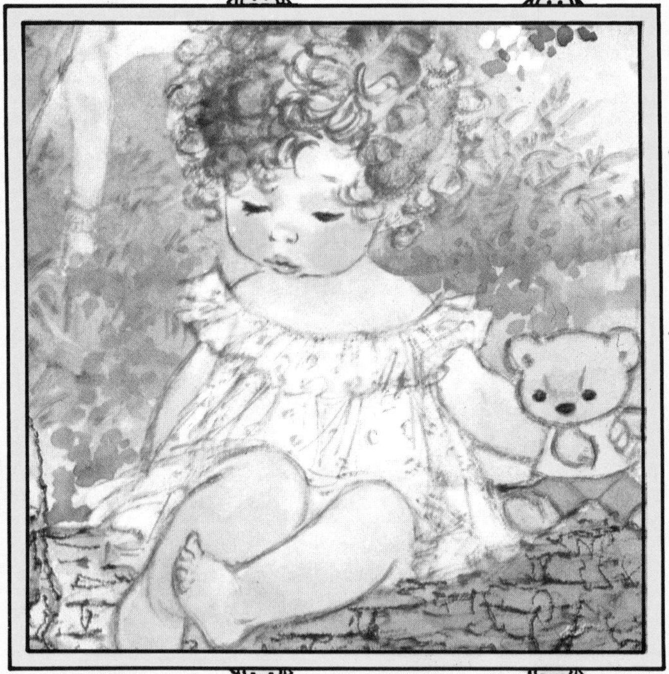